GOSCINNY AND UDERZO
PRESENT
AN ASTERIX ADVENTURE

ASTERIX AND SON

WRITTEN AND ILLUSTRATED BY UDERZO
TRANSLATED BY ANTHEA BELL AND DEREK HOCKRIDGE

HODDER AND STOUGHTON
LONDON   SYDNEY   AUCKLAND   TORONTO

British Library Cataloguing in Publication Data
Goscinny, René
  Asterix and Son
  I. Title   II. Uderzo, Albert
  741.5'944   PN6747

ISBN 0-340-33008-2

Original edition: © Editions Albert René,
Goscinny-Uderzo, 1983
English translation: © Editions Albert René,
Goscinny-Uderzo, 1983
Exclusive licensee: Hodder and Stoughton Ltd.
Translators: Anthea Bell and Derek Hockridge

First published in Great Britain 1983
Second impression 1983

Printed in Belgium for Hodder and Stoughton Children's Books,
a division of Hodder and Stoughton Ltd,
Mill Road, Dunton Green, Sevenoaks, Kent TN13 2YJ
by Henri Proost & Cie, Turnhout.

All rights reserved. No part of this publication may be
reproduced or transmitted in any form or by any means,
electronic or mechanical, including photocopy, recording,
or any information storage and retrieval system, without
permission in writing from the publisher.

GAULISH VILLAGE

COMPENDIUM

LAUDANUM

AQUARIUM

TOTORUM

ARMORICA

GAUL
(ROMAN CONQUEST)
50 B.C.

CELTICA

AQUITANIA

BELGICA

LUTETIA

PROVINCIA

The year is 50 BC. Gaul is entirely occupied by the Romans. Well, not entirely . . . One small village of indomitable Gauls still holds out against the invaders. And life is not easy for the Roman legionaries who garrison the fortified camps of Totorum, Aquarium, Laudanum and Compendium . . .

a few of the Gauls

Asterix, the hero of these adventures. A shrewd, cunning little warrior, all perilous missions are immediately entrusted to him. Asterix gets his superhuman strength from the magic potion brewed by the druid Getafix...

Obelix, Asterix's inseparable friend. A menhir delivery-man by trade; addicted to wild boar. Obelix is always ready to drop everything and go off on a new adventure with Asterix – so long as there's wild boar to eat, and plenty of fighting. His constant companion is Dogmatix, the only known canine ecologist, who howls with despair when a tree is cut down.

Getafix, the venerable village druid. Gathers mistletoe and brews magic potions. His speciality is the potion which gives the drinker superhuman strength. But Getafix also has other recipes up his sleeve...

Cacofonix, the bard. Opinion is divided as to his musical gifts. Cacofonix thinks he's a genius. Everyone else thinks he's unspeakable. But so long as he doesn't speak, let alone sing, everybody likes him...

Finally, Vitalstatistix, the chief of the tribe. Majestic, brave and hot-tempered, the old warrior is respected by his men and feared by his enemies. Vitalstatistix himself has only one fear; he is afraid the sky may fall on his head tomorrow. But as he always says, 'Tomorrow never comes.'

THE SUN IS RISING OVER ASTERIX'S VILLAGE, AS USUAL. THE SCENE IS ONE OF PEACE AND SERENITY...

...DISTURBED, DESPITE THE FACT THAT DAY IS DAWNING, BY THE SNORES OF THE ONLY GAULISH ROOSTER WHO HAS ADENOIDS.

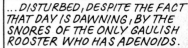

SNORT! ZZZ!

IT'S COCKCROW, YOU GOOSE! TIME TO TALK TURKEY.

YOU'RE IN A FOWL MOOD THIS MORNING!

TAP! TAP! TAP!

COCK-A-DOODLE-DOO

COME ON, GET UP! IT'S GOING TO BE A LOVELY DAY!

YAWN!

I HAD SUCH A FUNNY DREAM LAST NIGHT, ASTERIX!

SCRATCH! SCRATCH!

I DREAMED THE STORKS VISITED OUR VILLAGE, BRINGING THE BABIES PEOPLE HAD ORDERED, AND ONE OF THEM LEFT A BABY HERE BY MISTAKE!

SCRATCH SCRATCH!

DON'T SAY YOU STILL BELIEVE STORKS DELIVER BABIES!

WHY NOT? I DELIVER MENHIRS, DON'T I?

ONE OF THESE DAYS YOU AND I MUST HAVE A LITTLE TALK, OBELIX!

CREEEAK!

GA! GA!

GOO! GOO!

GURGLE!

I SEE YOUR PROBLEM, ASTERIX! WE MUST FIND OUT WHERE THE BABY COMES FROM AND WHOSE HE IS. IT'S URGENT!

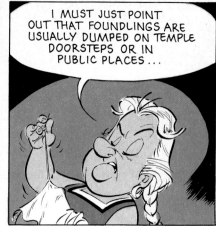

I MUST JUST POINT OUT THAT FOUNDLINGS ARE USUALLY DUMPED ON TEMPLE DOORSTEPS OR IN PUBLIC PLACES...

...SO THAT WHEN A BABY IS RATHER POINTEDLY LEFT OUTSIDE A BACHELOR WARRIOR'S HUT, PEOPLE ARE BOUND TO THINK THINGS!

THINGS? WHAT THINGS?

HEY! HANG ON! ARE YOU OUT OF YOUR MINDS?

TAP! TAP! TAP!

ONE MIGHT EVEN THINK MISTER ASTERIX WOULD HAVE NO TROUBLE IN FINDING THAT BABY'S MOTHER!

YOU DON'T MINCE YOUR WORDS, DO YOU? SHUT UP, OR I'LL MAKE MINCEMEAT OF *YOU!*

CALM DOWN! WE MUSTN'T GET UPSET!

ASTERIX! COME QUICK!!!

THAT'S OBELIX CALLING ME!!!

ASTERIIIIIIX! MOOOOOOO! DING DING DING!

AND IT LOOKED LIKE BEING SUCH A LOVELY DAY!

AVE, GAULS!

??!

I AM CRISMUS CACTUS, PREFECT OF GAUL, AND I HAVE COME TO INVESTIGATE THE WHOLE OF THIS CONQUERED TERRITORY AND TAKE A CENSUS OF THE GAULISH VILLAGES!

YOU'VE GOT ONE THING WRONG, ROMAN! THIS VILLAGE STILL HOLDS OUT AGAINST THE INVADERS!

AND WE'RE THE ONES DOING THE INVESTIGATING!

WE'LL SEE ABOUT THAT! READY MEN? AT THE WORD...

THIS IS A GREAT START TO OUR INVESTIGATIONS, ASTERIX...

GLUG! GLUG! GLUG!

PATCHAC!

SIGNA INFERRE! PRAEGE! CONCURSU! AD GLADIOS! INFESTIS PILIS!*

*FORWARD! MARCH! CHARGE! TO ARMS! TAKE AIM!

DISMOUNT!

BONK!

SINCE WE'RE MAKING INVESTIGATIONS, DO YOU HAPPEN TO KNOW OF ANY ROMANS WHO ABANDONED THEIR BABY OUTSIDE ASTERIX'S HUT?

DON'T BOTHER, OBELIX. ANYONE CAN SEE THEY'RE NEW TO THESE PARTS! LET'S GO TO COMPENDIUM!

!!!

WELL, NOW I KNOW ENOUGH TO GO BACK TO CONDATUM.*

*RENNES

RAISE THE ALARM!

CLOCK!

I DO LIKE YOUR TACT AND DELICACY, ASTERIX!

CRASH!

I TRY NOT TO BE A CRASHING BORE MYSELF WHEN I PAY CALLS!

HA, HA! GA!

HERE, WHAT'S THE IDEA?

WE'RE INVESTIGATING! ONLY PASSING THROUGH!

WELL, THERE'S NO CALL TO MAKE US PASS OUT!

PAF!

PIF!

DO YOU REGOGNIZE THIS BABY?

I'VE RECOGNIZED FOURTEEN BABIES WAITING FOR ME BACK IN ROME, BUT I'M ALMOST CERTAIN THAT'S NOT ONE OF MINE!

LET'S TRY THE CAMP OF LAUDANUM...

BUT IN THE CAMPS OF LAUDANUM...

...AND TOTORUM, THE INVESTIGATIONS GET NOWHERE.

SO THAT'S WHAT THEY CALL AN OPINION POLL?

16

MEANWHILE, AT CONDATUM, IN THE RESIDENCE OF THE PREFECT OF ARMORICA...

QUICK! SEND A MESSENGER OFF TO ROME!

DON'T BOTHER, CACTUS!

BRUTUS!?

THAT'S RIGHT! I'VE COME FROM ROME SPECIALLY TO HEAR THE LATEST ABOUT OUR LITTLE AFFAIR!

JUDGING BY YOUR SLOVENLY APPEARANCE, CONTACT WITH THE LOCAL BARBARIANS IS BAD FOR YOU!

CONTACT WITH THEIR FISTS IS! THIS INVESTIGATION YOU WANTED MADE IS A RISKY BUSINESS!

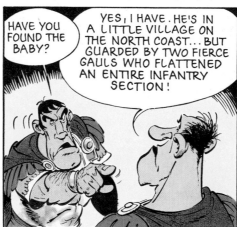

HAVE YOU FOUND THE BABY?

YES, I HAVE. HE'S IN A LITTLE VILLAGE ON THE NORTH COAST... BUT GUARDED BY TWO FIERCE GAULS WHO FLATTENED AN ENTIRE INFANTRY SECTION!

HMM... CAESAR'S OFTEN TOLD ME ABOUT THAT VILLAGE OF CRAZY BUT INDOMITABLE GAULS WHO GET THEIR STRENGTH FROM DRINKING MAGIC POTION!

BUT I'LL HAVE THAT BABY EVEN IF I HAVE TO PUT ALL GAUL TO FIRE AND THE SWORD.!!!

LUCKILY, SOME WAY OFF...

COME ON, SON, TRY YOUR LEGS OUT!

GA!

LOOK, ASTERIX! HE KNOWS HIS HOME ALREADY!

BANG!

Z!

JUST LIKE ME AT HIS AGE!

I WONDER IF WE'RE SETTING THAT CHILD A GOOD EXAMPLE?

AGA!

17

LATER... WELL, THE DOOR'S REPAIRED, THE BABY'S ASLEEP, AND DOGMATIX IS ON GUARD. SO LET'S GO AND DISCUSS THE SITUATION WITH CHIEF VITALSTATISTIX!

I'VE GOT TO DELIVER A MENHIR TO BUCOLIX FIRST!

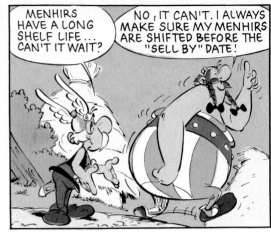

MENHIRS HAVE A LONG SHELF LIFE... CAN'T IT WAIT?

NO, IT CAN'T. I ALWAYS MAKE SURE MY MENHIRS ARE SHIFTED BEFORE THE "SELL BY" DATE!

SO THE ROMANS KNOW THE BABY IS HERE, AND THIS FAKE CENSUS OF THEIRS SUGGESTS THAT THEIR INTENTIONS AREN'T ENTIRELY HONOURABLE!

BUT WE STILL DON'T KNOW WHY SOMEONE CHOSE OUR VILLAGE AS THE PLACE TO LEAVE THE BABY.

I THINK I KNOW WHY!

THE BABY MUST NEED PROTECTION FROM THE ROMANS... AND OUR VILLAGE IS THE ONE SAFE PLACE WHERE ROMANS WOULD NEVER DARE TO COME!

14A

CRAAASH! ? ?

ASTERIX, SINCE I'M GOING TO SEE BUCOLIX ANYWAY, WOULD YOU LIKE ME TO PICK UP ANOTHER COW FOR THE LITTLE LAD?

OBELIX, MY BOY, I WISH TO GOODNESS YOU'D TAKE YOUR MENHIR OFF WHEN YOU COME INDOORS!

BUT, CHIEF, MENHIRS ARE HIGH FASHION INDOORS AS WELL AS OUT!

TOO HIGH FOR *MY DOOR* BY HALF, YOU IDIOT!

14B

18

DOGMATIX AND THE BABY HAVE GONE!!!

QUICK! WE MUST GO AND LOOK FOR THEM!

I CALL IT DISGRACE-FULL!

NAUGHTY LITTLE BOYS LIKE THAT OUGHT TO BE KEPT INDOORS!!!

WELL, THE FACT IS, WE DID...

...I DON'T GET IT! I SIMPLY SNEEZED, I OPENED MY EYES... AND LOOK!!

?

WE'LL HAVE TO FIND HIM BEFORE HE GETS A FIST IN EVERY DOOR IN THE VILLAGE!

16A

I'VE SPOTTED HIM! HE'S AT GETAFIX'S DOOR!

WOOF! WOOF!

COME IN!

TAP!

WOOF! GRRR! WOOF!!

? ?

?

WAAAAH!

ARF! ARF! ARF!

IS SOMETHING UP, ASTERIX?

YES ...THE EFFECT OF THE MAGIC POTION! IT'S WORN OFF THE BABY AT LAST. NOW FOR SOME PEACE AND QUIET!

WAAAH!

HARF! HARF! HARF!

16B

BUT IN CONDATUM...

SO NOW YOU KNOW THE DREADFUL SECRET OF THAT CHILD'S BIRTH, CACTUS!

AND YOU ALSO KNOW THE EQUALLY DREADFUL SECRET OF MY PLAN! IF YOU BETRAY ME, IT WILL BE THE WORSE FOR YOU!

WHAT, ME, BETRAY YOU? DO I LOOK LIKE A TRAITOR?

YES! BUT I HAVE NO CHOICE. SO IF YOU SERVE ME WELL, YOU'LL GET THAT SEAT IN THE ROMAN SENATE YOU'VE BEEN WANTING SO LONG!

I'D SELL MY MOTHER AND FATHER TO SERVE YOU IF I HAVEN'T DONE THAT ALREADY, O BRUTUS, SON OF CAESAR!

ONLY ADOPTED SON OF CAESAR, AND ALL I'M ASKING YOU TO DO IS BRING ME THAT BABY!

I HAVE AN IDEA!

FLOP!

WAAAH!

ASTERIX, SUPPOSE I GAVE HIM JUST ONE TINY DROP OF MAGIC POTION, MAYBE HE'D...

YOU'LL DO NO SUCH THING! YOU TWO HAVE CREATED ENOUGH HAVOC ALREADY!!!

ALL RIGHT, ALL RIGHT, I GET THE IDEA! MUSTN'T TREAT THIS PLACE LIKE HOME, MUST WE, DOGMATIX?

WAAAAH!

!

WAAAH!

HEY... HE'S LEFT ME HOLDING THE BABY! OH, VERY CLEVER, MISTER OBELIX!

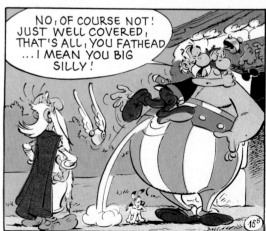

22

MEANWHILE, NOT FAR FROM THE VILLAGE...

O MARCUS JUNIUS BRUTUS, SINCE WE WANT OUR HQ NEAR THE INDOMITABLE GAULS, WHY DON'T WE USE ONE OF THE FORTIFIED CAMPS SURROUNDING THEIR VILLAGE?

BECAUSE CAESAR MIGHT GET TO HEAR OF IT, AND I'M NONE TO KEEN TO HAVE HIM ASKING ME WHAT I'M DOING HERE IN ARMORICA!

HALT! WE WILL PITCH CAMP HERE!

AND ONCE AGAIN WE ARE PRIVILEGED TO WATCH THE MANOEUVRES OF THE ROMAN ARMY. WHILE THE SAPPERS DIG A FOSSA (DITCH) AND RAISE AN AGGER (RAMPART)...

... THE WOODCUTTERS GO TO CHOP DOWN TREES ...

... FOR THE CARPENTERS TO BUILD THE VALLUM (FENCE).

AT LAST THE CAMP IS READY. THE GENERAL AND HIS MEN ARE ABOUT TO ENTER IN REVIEW ORDER, THUS SYMBOLIZING THE MIGHT OF THE ROMAN ARMY, THE BEST-DISCIPLINED FIGHTING FORCE IN THE WORLD...

?

... ALTHOUGH SOMETIMES...

WHAT'S THAT?

MY TENT! I CAN'T STAND THE WAY THE OTHERS SNORE IN BED!

HERE'S ODORIFERUS, THE LEGIONARY I MENTIONED, O BRUTUS!

HOW DID YOU KNOW WE WERE LOOKING FOR A BABY, ODORIFERUS?

I SORT OF, LIKE, HEARD THE PREFECT MENTION IT TO THE CENTURION AT AQUARIUM, O GENERAL, AND I, LIKE, Y'KNOW NEARLY BROUGHT YOU THE BABY BACK!

BONG

SO WHAT STOPPED YOU?

HE DID! HE SORT OF TOOK ME FOR A RATTLE, Y'KNOW, AND THEN HE, LIKE, SWUNG ME AROUND OVER HIS HEAD, O GENERAL!

YOUR MAN SEEMS TO HAVE HAD A KNOCK ON THE CAPUT*!

BUT HE'S NOT QUITE KAPUT... AND HE MAY YET BE USEFUL!

* ROMAN HEAD.

WELL, IF THIS BABY LIKES PLAYING WITH RATTLES, YOU CAN TAKE HIM SOME, ODORIFERUS! DISGUISE YOURSELF AS A GAULISH PEDLAR AND INFILTRATE THE VILLAGE OF THE INDOMITABLE GAULS! THEN YOU CAN EASILY SNATCH THE BABY AND BRING HIM BACK TO US!

IF YOU AGREE, AND SUCCEED, YOU'LL GET TO BE OPTIO!

AND IF I, LIKE, SAY NO, Y'KNOW?

21A

THEN YOU'LL, LIKE, GET TO BE DINNER FOR THE LIONS IN THE CIRCUS, *Y'KNOW!*

LATER...

DIDN'T YOU READ THE NOTICE? NO PEDLARS OR CIRCULARS IN THIS CAMP!

POC!

THE DISGUISE IS PERFECT... IT'S EVEN TAKEN IN THE SENTRY!

AND TO THINK I, LIKE, JOINED UP BECAUSE OF THE SMART UNIFORM!

LATER STILL, JUST OUTSIDE ASTERIX'S VILLAGE...

PAF!

GET OUT! NO PEDLARS OR CIRCULARS IN THIS VILLAGE!

21B

25

STOP HIM! STOP HIM! PROTECT ME!

ODORIFERUS, COME DOWN! AND THAT'S AN ORDER!

NO! NOOOO! I'D RATHER, LIKE, GO TO THE CIRCUS!

I HARDLY HAD TIME TO SPOT YOUR LITTLE FRIEND... BUT HE WAS AFTER THE PEDLAR, AND THE PEDLAR WAS IN SUCH A STATE HIS HAIR, BEARD AND MOUSTACHE HAD ALL DROPPED OUT!

QUICK, OBELIX! WE MUST FIND THAT BABY!

DOGMATIX IS ALREADY ON HIS SCENT!

SNIFF! SNIFF!

KEEP OUR BOARS ON ICE FOR US, FOTOGENIX. WE WON'T BE LONG!

THAT PEDLAR WAS NO MORE A GAUL THAN I'M A ROMAN! HE CAME TO KIDNAP THE BABY!

SNIFF! SNIFF!

IT'S A FUNNY THING, THE ROMANS BEING SO KEEN TO GET HOLD OF THAT CHILD!

YES, IT'S AS I ALWAYS THOUGHT.

WHAT IS?

THESE ROMANS ARE CRAZY!

TAP! TAP! TAP!

HERE HE IS, OBELIX! DOGMATIX HAS FOUND THE BABY!

DID YOU THINK HE WOULDN'T?

WOOF! WOOF!

HE'S FAST ASLEEP! WE MUSTN'T WAKE HIM!

I THINK HE'S DIGESTING THE PEDLAR!

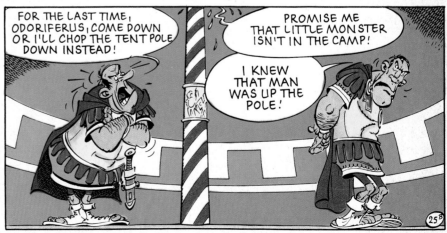

FOR THE LAST TIME, ODORIFERUS, COME DOWN OR I'LL CHOP THE TENT POLE DOWN INSTEAD!

PROMISE ME THAT LITTLE MONSTER ISN'T IN THE CAMP!

I KNEW THAT MAN WAS UP THE POLE!

NOW, DRINK THIS PICK-ME-UP AND TELL US WHAT HAPPENED, ODORIFERUS!

I, LIKE, SORT OF WON THE GAULS' CONFIDENCE, Y'KNOW, AND THEY GAVE ME THE BABY TO LOOK AFTER...

I WAS GOING TO CARRY HIM OFF WHILE THEY WERE OUT, BUT THAT LITTLE MONSTER HAS, LIKE, SUPERHUMAN STRENGTH, Y'KNOW, AND WHENEVER HE SEES ME HE SORT OF GOES INTO THE SAME ROUTINE, HE TAKES ME FOR A RATTLE AND...

HERE WE GO AGAIN!

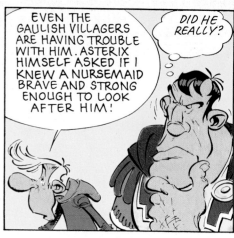

EVEN THE GAULISH VILLAGERS ARE HAVING TROUBLE WITH HIM. ASTERIX HIMSELF ASKED IF I KNEW A NURSEMAID BRAVE AND STRONG ENOUGH TO LOOK AFTER HIM!

DID HE REALLY?

I THINK I'VE, LIKE, EARNED PROMOTION TO OPTIO!

YOU? YOU'VE FAILED IN YOUR MISSION. THINK YOURSELF LUCKY NOT TO BE SERVED UP TO THE LIONS IN THE CIRCUS MAXIMUS!

I DIDN'T, LIKE, KNOW THESE PARTS BEFORE, BUT I WON'T BE SORT OF FORGETTING THE DISCOVERY OF ARMORICA IN A HURRY!

WHAT HE SAID ABOUT THE NURSEMAID GAVE ME AN IDEA! WHY DON'T **WE** SEND ONE TO THE VILLAGE?

PAF!

BECAUSE WE HAVEN'T GOT ANY NURSEMAIDS IN THE ARMY, THAT'S WHY!

YES, WE HAVE... YOU!

WHAT DO YOU MEAN, ME?

THINK, CACTUS! THAT LUNATIC OF YOURS WAS WELL AND TRULY PUT THROUGH IT BY THE GAULS. WE MUST REMAIN THE ONLY ONES IN THE SECRET. AND IF YOU REALLY WANT THAT SEAT IN THE SENATE...

WELL, PROMISE ME NO ONE WILL GET TO KNOW, ANYWAY!

LATER...

AVE, GORGEOUS! LIKE A BIT OF SLAP AND TICKLE?

SLAP!

BY ZHUPITER! THAT'SH GOING A BIT TOO FAR!

IT WORKS! EVEN THE SENTRY WAS TAKEN IN!

31

(FALSETTO) MY NAME IS ASPIDISTRA, AND I HEARD YOU WERE LOOKING FOR A NURSE. I'M A VERY EXPERIENCED NURSEMAID!

?!

BUT YOU'RE NOT ONE OF OUR VILLAGERS... HOW DID YOU KNOW I WAS LOOKING FOR A NURSE?

(FALSETTO) OH, THESE THINGS GET AROUND THE LEGION...I MEAN THE REGION! SPECIALLY WHEN IT'S SOMETHING TO DO WITH THE BOLD AND FAMOUS WARRIOR ASTERIX!

!?

HOW ABOUT ME? DO THEY KNOW ABOUT *ME* IN THE REGION?

?

(FALSETTO) CAN I REALLY BE SPEAKING TO OBELIX, THE HANDSOME AND SEDUCTIVE MENHIR DELIVERY MAN?

HOWEVER DID YOU GUESS?

AND DID YOU ALSO HEAR THAT THE CHILD IN QUESTION IS... ER...RATHER A HANDFUL?

(FALSETTO) I'VE THUMPED ...THAT'S TO SAY, I'VE BROUGHT UP WORSE HANDFULS, I'M SURE!

28

WE CAN ALWAYS TRY. GO ON, THEN, BUT DON'T SAY I DIDN'T WARN YOU!

FUNNY... I HAVE A FEELING I'VE SEEN HER FACE SOMEWHERE BEFORE!

MAYBE SHE'S NO MORE A NURSE THAN THAT MAN WAS A PEDLAR... WHAT DO YOU THINK OF HER, OBELIX?

A WOMAN OF TASTE AND DISCERNMENT!

WOMAN OF TASTE OR NOT, WE'D BETTER WATCH OUT!

TCHAC!

I DID WARN YOU! HE'S IMPOSSIBLE!

OH, I'M NOT RATTLED! I GOT OFF TO A FLYING START!

28

UNDER THE LANTERNA, BY THE CASTRA*GATE... MY LILIUM OF THE LANTERNA LIGHT, MY OWN LILIUM MARLENA!

I DON'T THINK SHE'S MUCH BETTER THAN CACOFONIX!

BARBARIANS! YOU'RE ALL BARBARIANS!

LOOK, YOU CAN TELL THE BABY DOESN'T LIKE YOU MUCH!

A LITTLE LATER...

HE'S DROPPED OFF AGAIN! IT'S ALL RIGHT, YOU CAN LEAVE HIM TO ME NOW!

JUST ONE THING... HOW DO YOU COME TO KNOW THESE SOLDIERS' SONGS?

*LATIN: BARRACKS.

ER...A CHILDMINDER'S JOB DOESN'T PAY MUCH, SO I TOOK TO MINDING A ROMAN ARMY CANTEEN TOO. THERE ARE WAYS AND MEANS OF MOONLIGHTING, AND THAT'S MINE...

...AND THAT WAY I GOT TO BE A MINE OF INFORMATION ON THE ARMY!

OH, WON'T I JUST HAVE EARNED MY SEAT IN THE SENATE!

WAAAH!

WELL, YOU'RE NEEDED AS A CHILDMINDER NOW!

31A

OH, OH, OH, IT'S A LOVELY BELLUM...

COME ON, OBELIX! LET'S FIND SOMEWHERE QUIETER!

OH, GOOD WORK, VITALSTATISTIX! MARVELLOUS, I CALL IT!

WHAT? WHAT HAVE I GONE AND DONE NOW?

YOU'RE CHIEF OF THIS VILLAGE... YOU LET A WOMAN FROM OUTSIDE COME AND LIVE UNDER A BACHELOR'S ROOF? OH, THAT'S GREAT!

BUT PEDIMENTA DEAR, SHE'S ONLY A NURSE FOR THE BABY!

EXACTLY! SUCH PROMISCUITY! SHOCKING!

I'M NOT ENJOYING THIS ADVENTURE VERY MUCH, OBELIX!

OH, IT'LL BE ALL RIGHT! IT'S SURE TO END WITH A BANQUET UNDER THE STARRY SKY, SAME AS USUAL!

31B

35

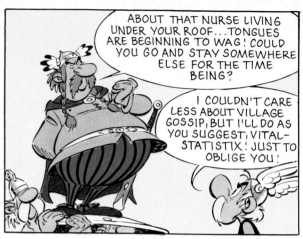

NEXT MORNING...

OH, I **WILL** HAVE EARNED THAT SEAT IN THE SENATE, AND NO MISTAKE!

GLUG! GLUG! GLUG!

BUT FOR THE EFFECTS OF THAT WRETCHED POTION, I'D TUCK HIM UNDER MY ARM AND MAKE OFF WITH HIM NOW!

BURP!

PAT! PAT! PAT!

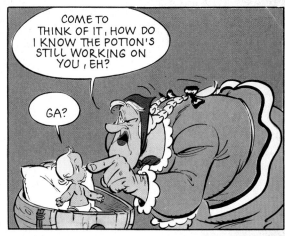

COME TO THINK OF IT, HOW DO I KNOW THE POTION'S STILL WORKING ON YOU, EH?

GA?

GA!

CLOCK!

33A

EVERYTHING OKAY?

SORT OF... ARE THE EFFECTS OF THAT MAGIC POTION GOING TO LAST MUCH LONGER?

THAT DEPENDS! JUDGING BY OBELIX, THEY COULD LAST FOR EVER!

AND SO, A LITTLE LATER...

WELL, I'M NOT GOING TO STICK AROUND IN THIS ROTTEN VILLAGE FOR EVER, WEARING THESE ROTTEN CLOTHES AND PLAYING THIS ROTTEN PART!

TOO BAD! I'LL RISK IT!

WHERE ARE YOU GOING, GORGEOUS?

ER... I'M GOING INTO THE FOREST TO PICK MUSHROOMS!

?

WAAAH!

33B

37

PACK UP YOUR TROUBLES IN YOUR OLD SARCINA* AND SMILE, SMILE, SMILE...♪

?!

SO NOW WE'RE OUT OF SIGHT OF THE VILLAGE...

*LATIN: KIT-BAG.

...I'LL MAKE STRAIGHT FOR THE CAMP!

WHERE ARE YOU GOING, OBELIX?

I'M DELIVERING A MENHIR TO BUCOLIX. THAT BABY HAS A GOOD APPETITE...HE'S COSTING US MANY A MENHIR!

I'LL COME WITH YOU!

I THOUGHT WE'D BE BETTER OFF WITH A NURSE. THEY USUALLY PROVIDE THE MILK, BUT THIS ONE DOESN'T SEEM TO.

34ª

IF YOU'RE LOOKING FOR THE BABY AND HIS NURSE, THEY'VE GONE INTO THE FOREST TO PICK MUSHROOMS!

QUICK, OBELIX! I'VE GOT A NASTY FEELING...

KEEP MY MENHIR ON ICE, FOTOGENIX! WE SHAN'T BE VERY LONG!

OUF!

SNIFF! SNIFF!

PHEW! THAT'S A WEIGHT OFF MY MIND!

GA!

MY MIND?

THROWING YOUR WEIGHT AROUND, EH? WAIT TILL I CATCH YOU, YOU ✳☸@°⚡!

34B

HELP! HELP! SAVE ME!

YESH, BY ZHUPITER! COME TO MY...

...ARMS!

SPLATCH!

DON'T BE RIDICULOUS, CACTUS! I ORDER YOU TO COME DOWN!

PROMISE ME HE ISN'T IN THE CAMP!

TOO BAD! SO I WON'T GET TO BE SENATOR... BUT DON'T ANYONE EVER MENTION THAT MONSTER TO ME AGAIN!

NOW, NOW! WE'VE LOST A BATTLE, WE HAVEN'T LOST THE WAR!

36 A

I TOLD YOU I'D PUT ALL GAUL TO FIRE AND THE SWORD IF NECESSARY... **SO NOW LET'S LIGHT THE FIRE!!**

AND AT DUSK...

FANCY MAKING US HAUL THESE ROMAN RELICS UP, JUST TO SHOOT OFF A LOT OF FIERY ARROWS!

YES, IT'S A FLAMING NUISANCE!

ARE YOU REALLY GOING TO PUT ALL GAUL TO FIRE AND THE SWORD, BRUTUS?

WELL, THE VILLAGE OF THOSE INDOMITABLE GAULS WILL DO! I'M TOLD THE THATCH ON GAULISH HUTS BURNS FAST AND WELL.

THIS TIME THE ROMANS HAVE TURNED OUT MORE CUNNING AND PERSISTENT THAN USUAL!

SO WE MUST TAKE MORE CARE THAN USUAL!

AND GOSSIP LESS, TOO!

YOU **WOULD** KEEP A-HOLD OF NURSE AND YOU FOUND SOMETHING WORSE!

36 B

SO THEY ARE... AND AT DAWN...

COCK-A... COUGH-A... COUGH!

LOOK, ASTERIX! I'VE MET THE PEDLAR AGAIN!

AND I'VE MET THE NURSE!

IT'S A GOOD THING WE OUTNUMBER THEM, OR WE MIGHT HAVE BEEN MOVED!

PAF! PAF! PAF! PAF!

NOW, TELL ME WHAT REALLY BROUGHT YOU HERE, OR YOU'LL HAVE A FEW TROUBLES OF YOUR OWN TO PACK UP IN YOUR OLD SARCINA!

MERCY! I WAS ONLY OBEYING THE ORDERS OF CAESAR'S SON, BRUTUS!

AND WHERE IS BRUTUS?

ON THE BEACH! HE KNEW YOU'D SEND THE BABY TO SAFETY THERE!

QUICK, OBELIX! FOLLOW ME!

QUICK, DOGMATIX! FOLLOW US!

WOOF! WOOF!

WHERE'S THE BABY?

ASTERIX, I HAVE FAILED YOU! A ROMAN SNATCHED HIM AND TOOK HIM ON BOARD A PIRATE SHIP!

I CAN STILL SEE IT ON THE HORIZON!

DO YOU THINK YOU COULD SWIM OUT THAT FAR?

YOU REALLY DO ASK STUPID QUESTIONS SOMETIMES, ASTERIX!

SORRY. I WAS ONLY THINKING..

WELL, OF COURSE I CAN!

I DON'T KNOW WHAT I'D DO WITHOUT YOU, OBELIX!

ALL SORTS OF SILLY THINGS!

SPLOSH! SPLOSH! SPLOSH! SPL

SO WE'VE FIXED THE PRICE, THEN, ROMAN?

YES, BUT YOU DON'T GET PAID UNTIL WE DISEMBARK AT BRIVATES PORTUS*.

*BREST.

THAT'S OKAY! I'VE A WIFE IN EVERY PORTUS ... SO THAT SUITS MY BRIVATE LIFE!

THE LAD MUST BE WORTH A LOT!

EVEN MORE THAN YOU THINK!

SHIVER ME TIMBERS... IF HE'S THAT VALUABLE, I'VE A GOOD MIND TO KEEP HIM FOR MYSELF!

TWO SWIMMERS ON OUR WAVE-LENGTH!

?

TWO SWIMMERS? WHO ARE THEY?

GAULS! THEY'RE MAKING WAVES! WE'RE IN DEEP WATER!

!

41 A

SURELY YOU'RE NOT ABANDONING SHIP JUST BECAUSE OF TWO GAULS?

YOU DON'T KNOW US, YOU NEVER SET EYES ON US, AND NOW WE'RE QUITS, ROMAN!

YOOHOO!

GOO!

COME ANY CLOSER, AND IT WILL BE THE WORSE FOR THIS BABY!

OUCH! OW!

GRRRR!

41 B

CLEOPATRA!

?!

AMAZING! WHAT A SIGHT!

AND WHAT A NOSE!

MY SON? CAESARION? BUT I THOUGHT YOU WERE BOTH SAFE IN MY PALACE IN ROME!

DID YOU SAY SAFE?

AFTER YOU LEFT, THE VILLAINOUS BRUTUS MADE SEVERAL ATTEMPTS TO DO AWAY WITH CAESARION, HOPING TO BECOME SOLE HEIR TO YOUR PROPERTY AND YOUR FORTUNE!

SO I DECIDED TO SEND OUR SON AWAY TO THE ONE PLACE WHERE I COULD BE SURE HE WOULD BE SAFE: THE VILLAGE OF INDOMITABLE GAULS WHICH STILL HOLDS OUT AGAINST THE INVADERS!

ALL RIGHT, I KNOW!

ET TU, BRUTE?✱ YOU WILL LEAVE IMMEDIATELY FOR UPPER GERMANIA! IT HAS A NICE BRACING CLIMATE, AND THE BARBARIANS THERE WILL TEACH YOU MANNERS!

✱ YOU TOO, BRUTUS? CAESAR SOMETIMES REPEATED HIMSELF.

FORGIVE ME FOR TAKING ADVANTAGE OF YOU, ASTERIX!

OH, THAT'S ALL RIGHT! I'M HONOURED BY YOUR FAITH IN ME, QUEEN CLEOPATRA!

THE... THE BABY'S DISAPPEARED!

47

WOOF! WOOF!

HE'S GONE TO SLEEP UNDER A TREE AGAIN!

HE LIKES TREES, SAME AS DOGMATIX! IT'S A GOOD SIGN!

THEN I'LL HAVE SOLID GOLD TREES MADE FOR HIM!

O QUEEN CLEOPATRA, AND YOU TOO, CAESAR, WE'RE SORRY THAT WE CAN'T INVITE YOU TO CELEBRATE THIS HAPPY EVENT IN OUR VILLAGE, BUT IT'S BURNT TO ASHES!

BUT THIS IS THE END! SO WHAT ABOUT THE BANQUET?

I PROMISE YOU MY ENGINEERING CORPS WILL REBUILD YOUR VILLAGE!

AND I'LL HOLD A BANQUET FOR YOU ON BOARD MY GALLEY! IT'S THE LEAST I CAN DO!

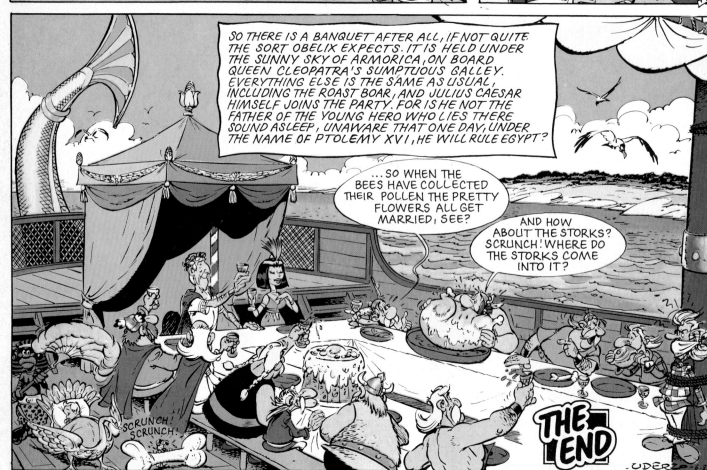

SO THERE IS A BANQUET AFTER ALL, IF NOT QUITE THE SORT OBELIX EXPECTS. IT IS HELD UNDER THE SUNNY SKY OF ARMORICA, ON BOARD QUEEN CLEOPATRA'S SUMPTUOUS GALLEY. EVERYTHING ELSE IS THE SAME AS USUAL, INCLUDING THE ROAST BOAR, AND JULIUS CAESAR HIMSELF JOINS THE PARTY. FOR IS HE NOT THE FATHER OF THE YOUNG HERO WHO LIES THERE SOUND ASLEEP, UNAWARE THAT ONE DAY, UNDER THE NAME OF PTOLEMY XVI, HE WILL RULE EGYPT?

...SO WHEN THE BEES HAVE COLLECTED THEIR POLLEN THE PRETTY FLOWERS ALL GET MARRIED, SEE?

AND HOW ABOUT THE STORKS? SCRUNCH! WHERE DO THE STORKS COME INTO IT?

SCRUNCH! SCRUNCH!

THE END

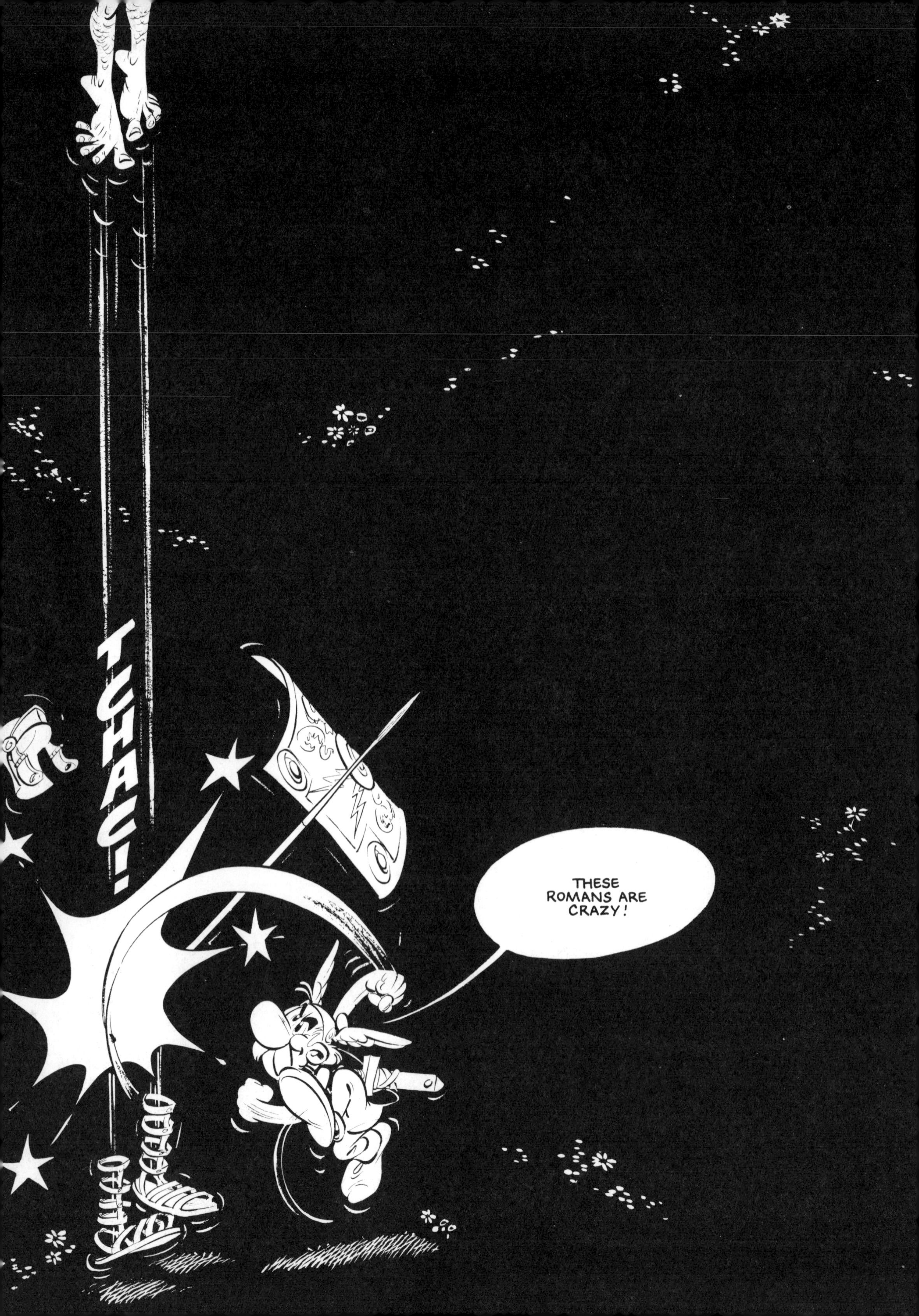

THHACK!!
THESE ROMANS ARE CRAZY!